for Janet and Gerald

Published by
PEACHTREE PUBLISHERS, LTD.
1700 Chattahoochee Avenue
Atlanta, Georgia 30318-2112

www.peachtree-online.com

First published in Great Britain in 2001 by Andersen Press

Color separated in Switzerland by Photolitho AG, Zürich.
Printed and bound in Singapore.

10 9 8 7 6 5

ISBN 13: 978-1-56145-250-7
ISBN 10: 1-56145-250-5

Cataloging-in-Publication Data is available from the Library of Congress

What's the Time, GRANDMA WOLF?

Ken Brown

Ω
PEACHTREE
ATLANTA

There's a wolf in the woods,
and everyone said,
    "She's big and she's bad, she's old
    and she's hairy. Best leave her alone,
    she's mean and she's SCARY!"

But we wanted to know,

so we crept a bit closer...

and Piglet, who's brave,
shouted...

"WHAT'S THE TIME, GRANDMA WOLF?"
    And she opened her eyes—
they were very, very big—and yawned,
"It's time I got up."

So we crept a bit closer, and Fawn, who's shy,
whispered, "What's the time, Grandma Wolf?"
And she pricked up her ears—
they were very, very big—and said,
"It's time I brushed my teeth."

So we crept a bit closer, and Crow,
who is noisy, squawked, "What's the
time, Grandma Wolf?"

And she took down a kettle—
it was very, very big—and said,
"It's time I scrubbed the stewpot."

So we crept a bit closer, and Squirrel,
who's sassy, squeaked, "What's the time,
Grandma Wolf?"
    And she fetched a sharp axe—
it was very, very big—and said,
"It's time to chop the wood."

So we crept a bit closer, and Badger,
who's bold, barked, "What's the time, Grandma Wolf?"
And she picked up two pails—
they were very, very big—and said,
"It's time I fetched some water."

So we crept a bit closer, and Duckling, who's silly, quacked, "What's the time, Grandma Wolf?"

And she looked down her nose—
it was very, very big—and said,
"It's time to light the fire!"

So we crept even closer, and Rabbit, who's reckless, giggled, "What's the time, Grandma Wolf?"

So we all settled down to a vegetable stew, and old Grandma Wolf, what did she do?

She read us our favorite story!